ScaredyBat
and the Sunscreen Snatcher

By Marina J. Bowman

Illustrated by Yevheniia Lisovaya

Code Pineapple

First paperback edition May 2020

Written by Marina J. Bowman
Illustrated by Yevheniia Lisovaya
Book design by Lisa Vega

ISBN 978-1-950341-13-9 (paperback color)
ISBN 978-1-950341-14-6 (paperback black & white)
ISBN 978-1-950341-12-2 (ebook)

Published by Code Pineapple
www.codepineapple.com

For all of you that have been stuck inside,
waiting for the special formula that will let
you go outside safely again.

Also by Marina J. Bowman

SCAREDY BAT

A supernatural detective series for kids with courage, teamwork, and problem solving. If you like solving mysteries and overcoming fears, you'll love this enchanting tale!

#1 Scaredy Bat and the Frozen Vampires

#2 Scaredy Bat and the Sunscreen Snatcher

#3 Scaredy Bat and the Missing Jellyfish

THE LEGEND OF PINEAPPLE COVE

A fantasy-adventure series for kids with bravery, kindness, and friendship. If you like reimagined mythology and animal sidekicks, you'll love this legendary story!

#1 Poseidon's Storm Blaster

#2 A Mermaid's Promise

Do you want to be a detective?

Get your FREE Custom Detective Guide to become the sleuth you were born to be!

GO HERE TO GET YOUR DETECTIVE GUIDE NOW:

scaredybat.com/book2bonus

Detective Team

Ellie
aka Scaredy Bat "the detective"

Jessica
"the courage"

Fez
"the heart"

Tink
"the brains"

Contents

Batty Bonuses

Can you solve the mystery?

All you need is an eye for detail, a sharp memory, and good logical skills. Join Ellie on her mystery-solving adventure by making a suspect list and figuring out who committed the crime! To help with your sleuthing, you'll find a suspect list template and hidden details observation sheets at the back of the book.

There's a place not far from here
With strange things 'round each corner
It's a town where vampires walk the streets
And unlikely friendships bloom

When there's a mystery to solve
Ellie Spark is the vampire to call
Unless she's scared away like a cat
Poof! There goes that Scaredy Bat

Villains and pesky sisters beware
No spider, clown, or loud noise
Will stop Ellie and her team
From solving crime, one fear at a time

Chapter One
Something Squishy

Ellie fought to catch her breath as she raced down the black-and-white tiled hall, frantically searching for room 302. She couldn't believe that she had slept in, especially on the first day of school.

CRASH!

Her pink backpack slammed to the ground with her not too far behind.

"I am so sorry!" said a high-pitched voice. "Here."

Ellie looked up at the blurry silhouette with which she had collided. She squinted to try to see who it was, but all she could make out was a flurry of long black ringlets and an extended hand with red nails. "Thank you,"

Ellie mumbled as she was helped to her feet.

"And you might need these," added the girl, holding out Ellie's glasses and backpack.

Ellie put her round glasses firmly back on the bridge of her nose and smoothed down her long, brown hair before grabbing her backpack. The girl she had run into not only had

a ton of black hair but also a thick dusting of freckles covering her cheeks and the bluest eyes Ellie had ever seen.

"I'm Ava. I'm new here, and I am completely lost. I'm really sorry again for crashing into you... I was just trying to find my homeroom."

Feeling less disoriented, Ellie gave the girl a big, fanged smile. "It's okay! I know how easy it is to get lost here. It's a pretty big place. What room are you looking for?"

Ava pulled out a yellow, crumpled sheet from her skirt pocket. "Umm, 302."

"Me too!" Ellie exclaimed. "Come on, I think it's just down here."

Ava followed Ellie around the corner, and sure enough, there stood the wooden door with "302" displayed in large, silver letters.

"I guess it was closer than I thought," said Ava. "What's your name?"

"Ellie!"

Ava smiled. "Well, Ellie, I really like your necklace." She pointed to the silver chain with the purple dragon pendant that hung around Ellie's neck. "Where did you get it?"

"It's actually--"

RING! The bell interrupted before Ellie could answer.

"We better go," Ellie said. "I hear that Mr. Bramble loves giving detention when you're late to his class."

"Oh, okay. Well, thanks for the help!" said Ava before rushing into the classroom.

Ellie found the desk with her name messily written with thick, black marker on a tented card, and she was excited to discover that she had been seated beside her best friend, Jessica. Jessica was doodling some fashion sketches in her black notebook. Her red curls bounced around slightly as she tilted her head from side to side to examine her latest creation. Finally, after a satisfied nod, she looked over at Ellie.

"I thought you got lost and were never coming," Jessica joked.

Ellie's breathing and heart rate finally began to slow down. She took in a deep breath before answering. "Well, you aren't wrong about the lost part. But it didn't help that I slept in." She

looked over at her best friend, expecting some sort of crack about her horrible sense of direction, but instead, Jessica was now focused on the other side of the classroom.

"Who is that?" Jessica whispered.

Ellie followed Jessica's stare to Ava, but she was promptly distracted by Fez enthusiastically waving at her. Ellie offered back a wave and a grin as her gaze trailed to a purple stain right below the bat silhouette on Fez's shirt. How that boy always found a way to get food stains on his clothes, she would never understand. Fez made his way across the class.

"Did you hear me?" Jessica asked.

"That's Ava," Ellie finally answered. "We sort of met in the hall earlier."

As Fez took his seat in front of the girls, a horrific garlicky scent filled Ellie's nose. She gagged before covering her nose with her silky shirt collar.

"Fez, why do you smell so much like gross garlic?" Ellie asked.

Fez looked down, sniffed his shirt sleeve, and shrugged. "I've been helping my dad with

his garlic dressing recipe for the Garlic Festival tomorrow."

"Well, you stink!" exclaimed Jessica, followed by a short cough. "I much prefer the blood orange salsa your dad made for the barbecue yesterday."

"It's nothing personal," added Ellie. "Most vampires hate the smell of garlic. But I totally loved your dad's red beans and rice!"

Fez smiled. "Yeah, he went all out for the end-of-summer barbecue." He uncrumpled a piece of paper from his pant pocket and smoothed it out on Ellie's desk. "Are you guys going to the Garlic Festival? We can get you nose plugs!"

Ellie opened her mouth to answer, but her heart jumped to her throat at the sight of a frizzy rainbow afro, a red nose, and a snowy-white face on the cover of the flyer. "Fez! Get that creepy clown away from me!" she shrieked.

Fez picked up the flyer, and his eyebrows slammed together in confusion. "He's not scary; look at that friendly smile." He turned

the flyer back around and held it up in front of Ellie's face.

She shut her eyes as tight as she could. "No! All clowns are terrifying. I. Hate. Clowns."

Fez looked at Jessica, who nodded. "It's true. She won't go near the circus when it comes to town. Not even for their blood pudding."

Fez recrumpled the flyer and stuck it back in his pocket as Jessica let out a short cough and cleared her throat.

"It's safe now," said Jessica. "Well, from the clown. Not the garlic smell."

Ellie slowly opened one eye and then the other, letting out a sigh of relief now that the clown was nowhere in sight.

"Clowns and garlic are both great! I think you guys are just being drama queens," said Fez.

"Agree to disagree." Ellie waved her left hand in front of her nose, trying to fan the garlic smell away while she used her right hand to dig in her pink backpack. "Now where did I put my lavender-scented Monster Spray...? That should help cover up the garlic."

Ellie's hand clutched something squishy and fuzzy that she didn't recognize. She pulled the mystery object out of the backpack and promptly dropped it, jumping out of her chair.

"EEK!" Ellie let out a startled shriek before turning into a bat.

POOF!

Chapter Two
The Mix Up

Ellie fluttered to the top of a wooden bookshelf and silently shook.

"Ms. Spark!" boomed Mr. Bramble from the front of the room. "If you are done with the theatrics, can we start class now?"

POOF! "No! Why are there clowns everywhere?" she squealed as she snapped back into her vampire form. "There's a giant clown head in my bag!"

Gasps and whispers flooded the classroom. Jessica reached down and lifted a squished clown's face off the floor.

"See!" said Ellie, still shaking and sitting on top of the bookshelf.

A laugh exploded over the chatter. "That's

not a clown head, it's just a silly mask."
The entire class broke out into giggles, and
Ellie's face grew hot with embarrassment.
Her attention darted to the boy responsible
for the statement. He sat in the back of the
classroom with his feet resting on his desk,

his curly black hair parted to the side, and a smug smile pasted on his face. "You're such a scaredy bat," he said.

Ellie had never seen this boy before, yet even he knew her nickname. "I am not!" she snarled. "Someone must have put that mask in there to scare me! And it looked a lot bigger and scarier when I was a small bat."

"Yeah, a *scaredy* bat!" the boy added.

Laughter filled the classroom, and Ellie looked down at his name card. *Jack Grinko.*

"That is enough!" snapped Mr. Bramble. "Miss Spark, take your seat." Ellie hopped down from the bookshelf and sat back at her desk, but not before sticking her tongue out at the mean mystery boy in the back. She didn't know who he was, but she didn't like him.

A hand slowly raised in the air on the opposite side of the class.

"Umm, excuse me, Mr. Bramble…" said a small voice. The whole class's attention turned to Ava. She pointed to her pink backpack. "I think me and Ellie got our backpacks mixed up."

Ellie looked down at the backpack next to her desk, noticing an unfamiliar lion emblem stitched onto the strap. "Oh."

Mr. Bramble ran a hand through his dark hair. "Alright, hurry up and switch back then."

"Sorry," Ava whispered as she rushed toward Ellie's desk. The two girls swapped backpacks, and Ava quickly returned to her seat.

Mr. Bramble gave them an outline of their year and started talking about their upcoming field trip to Jellyfish Lake the following week. "This is going to be an overnight trip," explained Mr. Bramble, "so I will need your permission slips as soon as possible. I should also mention that you will be allowed to choose your own bunk mate." This news sent the class into a flurry of whispers and excitement. Jessica gave Ellie a knowing look, and Ellie nodded back.

"Quiet down! I'm not finished," said Mr. Bramble. "Whomever you choose will also be your partner for a project related to Jellyfish

Lake. This can be a story, a presentation about the landmarks, or a paper on the area's history. You will have a lot of creative freedom for this project, but keep in mind that it will be worth thirty percent of your grade, so choose your partner wisely. I'm going to pass around the permission slips, so take a few minutes to pair up. If you can't find a partner, I can find someone for you."

Jessica gave Ellie a big smile that showed off her perfectly white fangs. "I am so excited!" she exclaimed. "My mom told me that a lot of celebrities like to vacation at Jellyfish Lake, so maybe we'll see one. I heard that last year that blond guy from the movie *Werewolf Island* vacationed there but forgot his sunscreen, so he ended up with permanent blue spots. It totally ended his acting career."

Ellie's mouth dropped open. "That's horrible! Do you know if it drained his transformational powers too?"

Fez turned around and leaned into the conversation. "Umm, why would a sunburn

leave blue spots? Or drain transformational powers?"

"That's just what happens," Ellie explained. "Vampires burn really easily in the sun, and if we do, we can be stuck with permanent blue spots. The sun can even drain our abilities. I mean, since I can't always control turning into a bat, I sometimes wonder if that would be such a bad thing…"

"Woah, I had no idea!" exclaimed Fez. "When I get a sunburn, my skin just turns red and peels."

"If you don't have enough sunscreen, make sure to get your parents to order more tonight," said Jessica.

Ellie smiled. "Don't worry. I just got a new bottle yesterday. It's right here." She began digging through her backpack, and slowly her smile disappeared. "Where is it?" She dumped the entire contents onto her desk, but there was no sunscreen.

"Did you forget it at home?" asked Jessica.

"No," said Ellie. "It's a brand-new bottle! If I don't find it, I am so dead."

Fez shrugged. "What's the big deal? Can't you just go to the store and buy a new one? I have a few bucks I can lend you." Fez pulled a few bills from his pocket.

"No, it's not like human sunscreen, Fez. Every vampire needs a special formula made because there are so many different skin types. That makes it super expensive."

Fez pulled a few more bills from his pocket.

"Like a hundred dollars expensive."

"Oh." Fez put his money away. "I can't help you there."

"I'm sure you'll find it," assured Jessica with a meek smile.

The lump in Ellie's throat grew larger, and her palms began to sweat. She hoped Jessica was right, because otherwise, Ellie was in serious trouble. She needed that sunscreen.

Chapter Three
Suspect Number One

"Maybe Ava has it!" Ellie looked across the room at Ava, who was talking and laughing with a short blond girl. Ellie sprang from her chair, raced across the room, and tapped Ava on the shoulder. "Do you have my sunscreen?" she asked in a quick huff, making her question sound like one long word.

"Umm, your sunscreen? I don't think so, sorry."

"You sure you didn't accidentally take it out of my backpack thinking it was yours?"

Ava shook her head. "Mine is in a special bottle, because I kept losing it and my parents were tired of paying for extra. See!" She unzipped the front pouch of her backpack and

pulled out a clear purple bottle attached to the bag with a gold chain and decorated with red gems.

Ellie's eyes lit up. "Wow, that is so pretty! Mine is just in a plain white bottle. You know, the usual one with the funny-looking sun on the front."

Ava nodded. "Yup! My brother uses that one." She pointed to Jack, the boy who had made fun of Ellie earlier. Ellie looked at Jack, who was twirling a string of pink gum hanging from his mouth around his finger. How could someone so mean be related to someone as sweet as Ava? Then again, you couldn't pick your siblings. Thoughts of Ellie's little sister, Penny, flooded her mind but were quickly pushed away with the sound of Ava's voice.

"Sorry again about the backpack mix-up," said Ava. "And sorry if my clown mask scared you. I wanted to say something sooner…" She lowered her voice to a whisper. "But Mr. Bramble kind of terrifies me."

Ellie smiled. "Don't worry, I think he scares

everyone." Both girls directed their attention toward the teacher writing down instructions on the large blackboard and shared a small laugh.

"Why do you have a clown mask?" Ellie asked.

"I'm volunteering at the Garlic Festival!" Ava said enthusiastically.

"Oh, well, have fun," said Ellie, not entirely sure why anyone would volunteer to be a creepy clown.

When Ellie got back to her seat, she beamed at a short boy with brown curly hair and glasses sitting beside her.

"Hey, Tink! Why are you so late?" she asked.

Tink adjusted the glasses on the bridge of his nose and groaned. "My alarm didn't go off and now I have detention. Detention on the first day of school. Can you believe it?" He sighed as he showed Ellie the pink detention slip.

"If it makes you feel better, I'm having a terrible day too. I was almost late, I accidentally turned into a bat, and I lost my sunscreen. I thought the new girl Ava had it, but nope."

"Sunscreen? Oh right, I've read about the blue dots thing." Tink paused for a moment in thought. "So, do you think you lost it or someone stole it? Kind of sounds like a mystery."

Ellie's eyes widened with excitement. It did sound like a mystery. This could be a chance for Ellie to put her detective skills to the test.

Mr. Bramble instructed everyone to go back

to their desks, and he started to explain more about the school year, but Ellie wasn't paying attention. She opened her small, purple notepad with the silver skeleton key on the front and wrote down something she learned from her favorite mystery series, *The Amazing Vampire Detective.*

Suspects must have two things: Access & Motive

She tapped her pencil lightly on the page as she thought about who could have taken her sunscreen. She had already ruled out Ava, so who else, and why?

1. *Pesky Penny – always stealing my stuff*
2. *Aliens – might need sunscreen when flying close to sun*
3. *Jack Grinko – seems like a bully*

Her sister Penny loved stealing Ellie's stuff, plus she was in some sort of weird "potion-making" phase where she snatched Ellie's lotions and hair products to pretend she was a witch creating magical brews. She was suspect number one, and Ellie was going to investigate her when she got home… But there was one small problem. Ellie looked out the window at the sun starting to peek out from behind the rain clouds.

Without her sunscreen, how was she ever going to get home?

Chapter Four
Saved by Science

Ring! The final bell of the day blasted through the hall, and Ellie emptied her backpack for the hundredth time—her sunscreen was still nowhere to be found.

She marched up to Jessica's locker and found her friend carefully applying pink lip gloss and looking into her small black locker mirror.

"Jess, I need to borrow your sunscreen."

"Sorry, I don't wear any," said Jessica with a shrug as she wiped a bit of gloss off with her finger.

Ellie's mouth gaped. "How!? You would have tons of blue dots if you didn't wear some."

Jessica closed her locker and shook her head. "Nope, not with the shot they came out with

last year. I get it once a month and I'm good to go! But hey, even if I did have sunscreen, you know it wouldn't work for your skin type."

Ellie groaned. "I wish I could get that shot, but my dad doesn't think it's as good as the sunscreen. He said he had a patient that had the shot but still ended up with permanent blue spots."

Jessica snickered. "Ellie, even if you were allowed to get the shot, you're terrified of needles." Ellie's face turned white at the thought. Jessica was right. "Anyway, I have to go meet my mom on the set of the new movie they're shooting in town, *Vampires in Paradise.* I'll see you tomorrow!"

Ellie waved at her friend and then dug in her backpack for something to protect her from the sun so she could get home. Nothing. She didn't need her sunscreen this morning because it was cloudy and raining, but now the sun was full blast. Continuing her search, she rounded the corner to the gym, and a sour smell hit her nose, while an odd sight caught her eye—a scrawny man with frizzy black hair

that everyone referred to as "Stinky Lou" was digging in a large garbage bin. No, he wasn't called Stinky Lou because he dug in the garbage. It wasn't what he usually did… or at least Ellie didn't think so. The truth was that Stinky Lou was a rare sight around town, and no one quite knew why he stank, but there were a couple of theories.

The simple one was that he never showered. But whenever Ellie saw him, he never looked

dirty—he just smelled awful. Another popular explanation was that he rubbed himself with garlic, wet dog fur, old socks, and rotten fruit so kids would leave him alone. And finally, there was a legend that the ghosts in his house put a curse on him that made him permanently stink. That was always the one Ellie chose to believe, even though deep down she knew it was kind of ridiculous. She gulped, quietly turned around, and headed back down the hall.

Ellie went to the science lab next and started rummaging through drawers and cabinets. She found beakers, funnels, and magnets, but nothing that would protect her from the sun. After what felt like her twentieth drawer, Tink walked into the classroom.

"Hey, Tink, aren't you supposed to be in detention?" asked Ellie.

Tink turned around. "Oh, hi, Ellie. Yeah, but after-school detention doesn't start until next week. What are you doing here?"

Ellie bit her bottom lip as she looked around the room. "I need to get home. I don't have my sunscreen, so I need something to cover

me and protect me from the sun."

Tink thought for a moment. "I have just the thing." He headed to a drawer at the front of the class and pulled out a large roll of tin foil. "It won't protect you from the heat, but it should save you from the sun."

"Done!" Ellie exclaimed. She held out her arms as Tink wrapped the tin foil around her body.

Crinkle! Crinkle!

"You sure found this quickly," Ellie said over the sound of the foil. "I had science in here last year, and I still don't remember where the goggles go."

Tink let out a small laugh. "Well, I guess I spend a lot of time here." His lips made a tight, straight line. Tink paused, and the crinkling of the foil followed. "When my foster mom gets busy with her wedding planning, I come here a lot just to fiddle around. It beats being bored at home... plus it can be lonely there sometimes."

"Oh, maybe you just need your own science lab at home," Ellie said, trying to lighten the mood a bit.

27

Tink's slight smile reappeared. "Oh, I wish! That's the dream."

Ellie smiled back. "Well, you can come to my house for dinner if you want."

"What are you having?"

"I think my Mom said that blood pudding was today's after-school snack, and liver, rare steak, and boiled beets were supper." Her mouth started to water just talking about it.

Tink's face turned green. "I think I am going to pass, but thanks anyway."

"Okay, but you're missing out!" Once her entire body was covered in multiple layers and the only parts of her showing were her eyes and mouth, she shifted her stiff body around.

"You sure about dinner?" she asked one last time.

"One hundred percent," said Tink. "But thanks anyway."

"Okay, well, thanks for your help!" With her shiny silver shell, she looked like she was wearing a bad Halloween costume. She crinkled her way out the door and began her run home.

Chapter Five
Polka Dot Potato

Crinkle! Crinkle!

Ellie ran through her front door, drenched in sweat, and leaned forward to catch her breath. She made it home, but she had never been so hot in her life. She raced to the kitchen trash can to begin peeling off the layers of shiny foil and found her pesky sister, Penny, sitting at the nearby table in the corner.

With her face full of pudding, Penny looked up at Ellie, who was now frantically trying to free herself from her silver shell. "You look like a baked potato!" Penny declared, shrieking with laughter.

Ellie paused her peeling efforts to shoot Penny a dirty look. "Yeah, well, at least I know

how to put food in my mouth and not all over my face."

Penny's smile quickly turned to a pout. "Mom! Ellie is being mean."

"Shhh!" Ellie urged. "Don't call Mom."

"Why not?" Penny crossed her arms.

"Because I said so."

Not pleased with that answer, Penny tried again. "Mom! Mom! MO--"

Ellie bolted to the table and covered her sister's mouth with her tinfoil-covered hand. "If you stop, I'll give you whatever you want."

Penny nodded in agreement after a couple seconds of thought, and Ellie slowly removed her hand.

"Why? You don't want Mom to know you're a big baked potato? Why *are* you a baked potato?"

"No more questions. What do you want me to give you?" asked Ellie.

Penny looked down at the full bowl of blood pudding set out at Ellie's spot and then back at her own, almost-empty bowl. "I want your blood pudding!"

"Fine."

"For the next month," Penny added.

Ellie's jaw dropped. "No way! I am not giving you my favorite food in the world for a whole month!"

Penny smirked. "Fine, then I'm telling. Mom! MO--"

"Argh! Two weeks, that's it!" Ellie shoved the bowl toward her sister, and it slid across the table. She couldn't risk her parents finding out that she had lost her sunscreen, especially since it was a new bottle. They could only afford one bottle per month because it was so expensive, and Ellie had just gotten her new one. Penny started shoveling the second bowl of pudding into her mouth.

"Did you take my sunscreen?" Ellie narrowed her eyes at her sister.

"Nope." Penny sputtered pudding across the table with her answer, and Ellie watched for her sister's signature lip twitch. Penny was a horrible liar whose lip always twitched when she was trying to hide the truth, but it was hard to see under the mess of pudding. Penny looked at Ellie and started laughing.

"What's so funny?" Ellie asked.

A dribble of pudding fell from Penny's mouth. "You also have polka dots. You're now the funniest potato ever!"

Ellie's eyes widened. "No!" She stumbled up the stairs to look in the bathroom mirror and found subtle green splotches sprinkled across her face. A wave of relief washed over her. Green meant that they would fade; it was only the blue ones that were permanent. Clearly, tinfoil wasn't enough protection, though. She had to find her sunscreen ASAP, and she knew exactly where to start looking.

Penny was her prime suspect. Her sister was always "borrowing" her stuff, so why should this be any different? Ellie pushed open her sister's door to find toys blanketing the floor. She didn't know how Penny ever found anything in this mess, and she certainly didn't know how she was going to find her sunscreen.

After rummaging through the toybox, under the bed, and in the closet, Ellie found a white plastic bottle hiding under a jean jacket. "Aha!" She looked at the yellow label, and her

heart raced with excitement as she recognized the quirky little sun logo with the straw hat and red sunglasses. This was definitely the specially formulated sunscreen, but was it hers? She flipped over the bottle, only to have the words "Made for Penny Spark" instantly crush her hope. She threw the bottle onto the pink coffin bed and grabbed the purple scarf that

she thought she had lost before heading to her own bedroom. No sooner did she enter her room than she heard her name.

"Ellie, dinner!" called Mom from downstairs. Ellie's stomach vibrated as it growled like a lion. She checked her mirror. The green splotches had faded but were definitely still there. Not wanting to answer sunscreen questions, she had to think of how to cover them.

"Ellie!"

And fast. "Coming!" Ellie called back. She spun in place a few times as she looked around for a possible solution. She wasn't allowed to wear makeup, and hoods only covered her hair. What was she going to do? Suddenly, the dark purple scarf in her hand caught her eye. *It might just work,* she thought. She wrapped it around her face a few times so only her eyes and mouth poked out. And when she looked in the mirror, she couldn't help but think she looked like a fashionable mummy.

"Ellie! It's getting cold," called Mom.

"Coming!" Ellie called back once again. The purple scarf would have to do.

She made her way downstairs, and a mixture of salty and sweet aromas wafted through the kitchen. Ellie casually sat down at the table, and all eyes fell on her as she looked down at her plate filled with liver, rare steak, and a seared cow's heart. "Wow, this looks really good!" she said.

Ellie's mom looked over at her husband. "Do you want to ask, or should I?"

Ellie's dad shook his head. "This is all yours." He returned to his plateful of vegetables.

"Why are you wrapped in a scarf?" Mom asked.

Ellie stuffed some liver into her mouth to buy herself more time to answer, but Penny was more prompt.

"I think she just likes dressing up. Earlier today she was a big baked potato!" Penny exclaimed. Ellie kicked Penny's leg under the table. "Ow!" Penny cried.

"What is going on?" asked Mom, crossing her arms over her chest.

Ellie swallowed her food. "Oh, um. I'm writing a paper on mummies and wanted to know what it feels like to be one. Don't you like it?"

Dad smiled. "That's my girl! Glad you're taking school so seriously."

Mom sighed. "Well, purple has always looked good on you. Must you wear your scarf at the table, though?"

"Yeah, must you wear *my* scarf at the table?" Penny echoed.

"This is my scarf!" Ellie sneered.

"Are you sure about that, polka dot potato?" Not wanting to risk a lecture on responsibility and sunscreen, Ellie gritted her teeth.

"I'll give it back to you when I'm done."

Satisfied with that answer, Penny happily went back to stuffing her face.

After getting through dinner with no more questions, Ellie headed back to her bedroom. She took a seat on her coffin bed beside the wall covered floor-to-ceiling with posters from detective movies and shows, mostly with her favorite detective, Hailey Haddie. She looked at the newspaper clipping with her, Tink, Jessica, and Fez smiling below the headline, "The Small Detective Team That Saved The Royal Vampire Wedding." Ellie smiled at the memory before focusing on a photo of Hailey Haddie. In the photo, Hailey was chewing a pen cap as she made a list of suspects. Ellie decided it was time to further examine hers.

1. *Pesky Penny — always stealing my stuff*
2. *Aliens — might need sunscreen when flying close to sun*
3. *Jack Grinko — seems like a bully*

Satisfied with her possibilities, she gave a nod as she read them over. But after thinking a bit more, she grabbed her pen and made a few changes.

1. ~~*Pesky Penny*~~ *(No sign of my sunscreen in her room)*
2. ~~*Aliens*~~ *(They fly so close to the sun they would need much stronger sunscreen)*
3. *Jack Grinko — seems like a bully*

She narrowed down to one suspect, Jack Grinko. He liked to be a bully, and this would be a great way to do it.

Jack was now her prime suspect.

Chapter Six
This Stinks

The next day, Ellie traded her tinfoil protection for her favorite turquoise trench coat, detective hat, wool mittens, the purple scarf, pants, and sunglasses. She loved the detective hat and coat together; however, the rest was way too hot and made the outfit clash. But she didn't care. She wasn't taking any chances.

As soon as she got to school, she ran into the brick building and threw off her itchy mittens and damp scarf. Losing her sunscreen in the winter would have been much easier, and a whole lot less sweaty. She made her way to the science lab to replace the tinfoil she'd borrowed and found Tink in the same spot she'd left him.

"Did you sleep here?" she joked.

40

Tink laughed. "No, when the janitor leaves, I have to, too. But I do have something for you!" He handed Ellie a small bottle. "I found this sunscreen recipe on the internet, and the reviews say it works great, but only for about twenty minutes."

Ellie broke into a big, fangy smile. "Thank you so much, Tink! This is so nice of you." She lunged toward her friend and wrapped her arms around him.

"You're welcome," Tink replied.

Ellie broke away from the hug and smoothed out her trench coat. "Hey, have you seen Fez and Jessica anywhere today? I want to talk to you guys about a sunscreen snatcher lead."

"Sunscreen snatcher?" asked Tink. Just as Ellie pulled out her notebook with the suspect list, a wave of noise washed in from outside. Ellie and Tink raced over to the window to see what all the fuss was about. Right in the middle of a group stood Fez and the mean kid from homeroom, Jack Grinko. Standing almost a foot taller than stout Fez, Jack towered over the boy. This made it easy to keep the mystery object he held just out of Fez's reach.

Jack dangled the white object, and Ellie's eyes bulged. "That's my sunscreen!" she exclaimed. But when she turned to look at Tink, he was nowhere in sight. Ellie snatched up the homemade sunscreen and began lathering herself with the thick lotion that smelled faintly of black licorice. Ellie gagged slightly.

She hated black licorice. She held her breath as she finished applying and raced outside.

She made her way to the scene to find Tink with his hands on his hips, standing beside Fez. With Tink being even shorter than Fez, freakishly tall and lanky Jack now looked like a giant.

"G- give it back!" Tink demanded in a shaky voice.

Jack laughed. "What if I don't? What's a little nerd like you going to do about it?"

Tink lowered his hands from his hips and sucked in a deep breath that puffed out his chest. "I'm going to... I'm going to..." He paused to think for a second. "I'm going to turn you blue!" He let out his breath in one big huff.

"Blue!?" Jack laughed. "How are you going to do that?"

Tink mumbled a few unclear words and looked down at the ground.

Jack's laughter was overpowered by the first bell. He walked over to Tink and looked him straight in the eye. "You're lucky you were saved by the bell, dweebs." Jack shoved the bottle into Fez's hands and took off.

Ellie rushed over to Fez and Tink. "Are you guys okay?"

"Yeah, are you okay?" echoed a soft voice behind Ellie.

Ellie turned. Ava was walking toward them. Tink and Fez nodded in unison. "I was just minding my own business when Jack decided to steal this," Fez said, showing off the white bottle.

"Wow," said Ava. "Jack can be such a jerk!"

Everyone agreed.

"I hardly know him, and I already don't like him," said Ellie.

"Same here," said Tink.

"Me too," agreed Fez.

Ava sighed. "Yup, he has that effect on people. Well, I should get to class. Glad you're okay!" And with that Ava gave a quick wave before rushing inside.

Fez's eyes were glued to Ava as she pranced off, and the white bottle slipped from his hand, crashing to the pebbly, gray gravel. "Oops."

"What is that, anyway?" asked Tink, looking at the bottle. Fez bent down and picked it up.

"My sunscreen!" cried Ellie, excitedly snatching the bottle from Fez's hand as he straightened.

A frown appeared on Fez's face. "I wish people would stop taking my garlic dressing like that! That's exactly what Jack did."

"Garlic dressing?" said both Tink and Ellie. Ellie read the label on the bottle: "Fitzgerald's Garlic Dressing – Entry #21." She flipped the bottle over to reveal a yellow garlic head wearing red sunglasses and a big smile.

"Oh." The corners of Ellie's mouth turned down. "It looked exactly like my sunscreen bottle. What is this?"

Fez beamed proudly. "My dad's entry to the dressing competition at the Garlic Festival! The garlic mixture still needed to cool before being added to the plain dressing base, so I agreed to bottle it and submit it to the festival after school. Doesn't it smell great?" Fez twisted the cap off the bottle, and the scent of garlic flooded the air.

"No, that's horrible!" Ellie shrieked.

"I think it smells delicious," Tink said, leaning closer. "Do I also smell paprika?"

45

"Yeah." Fez nodded enthusiastically. "I can't wait to snack on the extra bottle my dad left out for me."

Jessica walked up to the group wearing a leopard-print sweater and a big smile. "Hey, guys, didn't the first bell already ring— Oh. My. Gosh! What is that awful smell?" Jessica pinched her nose shut and backed away.

Ellie laughed. "See!" She pulled out her notepad from her pocket. "Okay, guys, my sunscreen is still missing. I wanted to talk to you about Jack as a suspect, but now I'm not so sure. I think he would have rubbed it in my face by now, but he could have made the switch when Ava and I collided in the hall. They *are* siblings, so maybe they're working together. What do you think?"

"I don't think so," Jessica answered in a nasally voice. "I was in class pretty early, and Jack was there the whole time."

"Oh." Ellie's shoulders slumped. "If Jack has an alibi, then I don't have any more suspects. Now I'm never going to find my sunscreen, and my parents are going to ground me forever."

Fez patted Ellie on the shoulder. "Now *this* stinks."

With her nose still pinched, Jessica continued to talk in a nasally voice. "Don't give up yet, Ellie! Speaking of things that stink, I saw Stinky Lou digging in the school garbage yesterday, and he's been spotted around town

pulling bottles of sunscreen from bins. Maybe he could be behind it?"

Ellie did an excited little hop. "Yes, I saw him randomly digging in the school garbage yesterday, too. Super suspicious. Do you really think he stole my sunscreen, though?"

"Well, he hardly ever leaves his house, so maybe he needs sunscreen to go outside more or something," Jessica said. The group nodded in agreement. It was possible.

"Let's check it out after school!" Ellie decided.

Satisfied with the new lead, Ellie updated her list.

1. ~~Pesky Penny~~ *(No sign of my sunscreen in her bedroom)*
2. ~~Aliens~~ *(They fly so close to the sun they would need much stronger sunscreen)*
3. ~~Jack Grinko~~ *(Just a big jerk, not a sunscreen snatcher)*
4. *Stinky Lou — seen taking sunscreen from trash & might need it to go outside more*

Chapter Seven
Upside Down

Jessica, Tink, and Ellie stood on the concrete steps of the old house on the corner of 4th Street. Fez went to drop off the garlic dressing at the festival, but he promised to join the group later.

When Ellie was younger, she would always hold her breath going by this house, because other kids said that ghosts lived there and you might inhale them. Being this close to the house, she suddenly believed it was haunted more than ever. If only she could hold her breath for more than a few seconds...

"You know what? My sunscreen isn't that important," Ellie said matter-of-factly. "Tink made me this weird licorice stuff that lets me

go outside for a bit. Let's go grab a bite to eat, I'm starving!"

Just as Ellie began to turn on her heel, Jessica grabbed her arm. "No, you need your sunscreen."

Ellie waved her off. "Nah. I can wait a few weeks for the new stuff."

Tink silently followed the conversation, shifting uncomfortably from one foot to the next. He had spent enough time with Jessica and Ellie to know not to get in the middle of their bickering.

"No, no, you cannot," Jessica said. "That trip to Jellyfish Lake is in one week, and you won't have your new sunscreen by then."

Ellie's face turned blank. She hadn't thought of that before.

"Do you really want to stay at school instead of going on the big trip?"

"Maybe it wouldn't be so bad…" Ellie started.

"Fine. Maybe I'll ask that new girl, Ava, to be my roommate."

Ellie's mouth gaped. "But I was going to be your roommate!"

"And I also learned recently that Jellyfish Lake is one of Hailey Haddie's favorite spots. So, who knows, she might be there."

Hailey Haddie was one of Ellie's all-time heroes, and Ellie didn't know what she would do if she missed the opportunity to meet her.

Tink finally decided to throw in a word. "It would be easier to have a partner that has actually experienced the trip, since we have to do an assignment on it after. And it would be a bummer to miss out on Hailey Haddie."

Ellie shot an unimpressed look at him, and Tink's gaze trailed away from her. "Just saying," he added.

"Fine!" Ellie exclaimed. "We're going to do this!" She marched up to the door and banged the metal knocker against the cracking wood. After her knocks were only answered with silence, she tried again. Over a minute passed, but there was still no answer.

"Maybe we should try again later," Tink offered. Just then, an orange cat raced up to the door and gave it a slight push. The big door slowly creaked open. Clearly pleased with his

actions, the kitty's tail waved from side to side in the air, and she slunk in.

"Hello? Hello!?" Jessica called through the front entrance. "Is anyone home?" The sound of her voice echoed back at her, but no one else answered.

"Maybe we should just go in," Ellie suggested. "I'm sure if Stinky Lou stole my sunscreen, he wouldn't risk bringing it out in public. Come on!" Before either of her friends could object or she could change her mind, Ellie entered the creepy house.

"Ellie. Ellie!" Tink and Jessica called after her in loud whispers, but she had already disappeared around the corner.

Ellie found herself in a large hallway filled with the smell of pinewood and lined with portraits of cats. Some were photos printed on canvas, while others were large oil paintings of cats in various costumes. There was even one particularly large artwork of a plump orange cat dressed as a clown. A large shiver made its way up Ellie's spine, and her arms broke out in goosebumps. There was something so creepy about clowns—especially cat clowns, apparently.

"Ellie!" came a loud whisper. Ellie jumped slightly and whipped her head around. Jessica and Tink had joined her inside the house. She waved before giving the cat portraits one last look.

Jessica came up beside her. "Wow, these are…" Jessica trailed off, not knowing how to finish her sentence.

"Kinda cool," offered Tink with a satisfied nod.

Jessica's jaw dropped. "Not the words I was going for."

"I really like this one." Tink pointed to a cat in a lab coat wearing goggles with beakers all around him.

"You would," said Jessica with an eye roll.

"Guys, we need to look for clues," Ellie interrupted. "Let's try the kitchen."

The trio found the kitchen through the living room. It was a lot less dusty than the rest of the house, and an assortment of lab equipment littered the center island. There were vials of

chemicals, beakers, a Bunsen burner, and tons of notes scattered everywhere.

"Maybe that scientist cat in the picture lives here," Jessica joked. But Ellie was already looking for clues, and Tink was too busy examining all the science stuff to hear her. Jessica joined the search with a sigh. "What exactly are we looking for?" she asked.

"A bottle of sunscreen with my name on it... or clues to help us find it," Ellie answered.

Jessica nodded and began lifting a stack of papers off the counter.

"Don't touch those!" Tink hissed. "They're probably in a very specific order. You have to be super careful around science experiments or you could ruin the whole thing."

Jessica dropped the papers in surrender and moved her search to another area of the kitchen. Ellie began opening the cupboards, which were mainly filled with glass containers and the occasional pot and pan. But then she opened a big drawer labeled "SUN."

"Look!" Ellie cried.

"Shhh!" hushed Jessica.

Ellie tried again in a whisper. "Look." She pointed at the drawer. There were over eighty white bottles neatly lined up in rows, all labeled with black marker.

"One might be yours," said Jessica before both girls started sifting through the collection.

CRASH! POOF!

The piercing sound of shattering glass made Jessica jump and instantly caused Ellie to turn into a bat.

"Sorry, that was just me," said Tink.

Jessica put her hands firmly on her hips. "Whatever happened to 'being super careful around science experiments,'" she said in a mocking voice.

BANG!

Suddenly the pantry whipped open to reveal a man hanging upside down by his feet, and he was staring directly at Tink and Jessica.

Chapter Eight
The Formula

Jessica shrieked and ran into Tink's arms. The upside-down man wore a stained lab coat and had some sort of metal helmet with wires strapped to his head. "What is going on?" the man asked. He flipped himself upright and walked over to the trembling duo before silently turning his attention to the shattered glass on the floor.

"You know, you really *do* need to be more careful around science equipment," he scolded before grabbing a nearby broom.

"We-we should go," Tink said, grabbing Jessica's hand.

"Not yet," said the man. "You break it, you clean it." He extended the broom toward Tink.

Tink shakily let go of Jessica's hand to grab the broom and began sweeping the mess.

"You're kinda sweaty," said Jessica, wiping her newly-released hand on her dress.

"Yeah, well, I nearly had a heart attack just now, so it makes sense," Tink muttered.

"Sorry if I scared you," said the man as he let out a breath before taking off his strange helmet device and sitting on a charred stool. "But what are you two doing in my house? Don't you know that you're trespassing?"

Tink nodded. "Yes, sir. We are very, very sorry."

"We were just looking for our friend Ellie's sunscreen," Jessica replied.

"Well, I hardly feel that is an excuse to break into my house. And shouldn't she be looking for her own sunscreen?"

Tink paused his sweeping efforts for a moment, and he and Jessica exchanged a look. "Well, she is..." said Jessica. *POOF!* Ellie appeared in the middle of the kitchen, causing the man to almost fall off his stool.

Ellie's cheeks flushed as she gave a small

wave and mumbled a soft, "Sorry." Strangely, Lou didn't smell bad today; in fact, he kind of smelled like warm apple cider with a hint of cinnamon.

"You kids are going to be the death of old Stinky Lou," said the man. The gang exchanged another round of looks with each other. "Yes, I know what everyone calls me," Lou said, confirming what they were all thinking.

"Why were you digging through the trash at our school yesterday?" Ellie inquired, placing her hands on her hips.

Lou pointed to his helmet on the counter. "I'm good friends with your science teacher, Mr. Crunkle, and he allows me to take my pick from the recycled electronics bin for my experiments."

Ellie took her hands off her hips, and her shoulders slumped. "So, you didn't steal my sunscreen?"

Lou let out a loud laugh that sounded like a small marble was clanking around in the back of his throat. "Why would I want your sunscreen? I have several dozen bottles over

there." He pointed to the open drawer. "You're welcome to help yourself."

Tink swept the glass into the dustpan and dumped it into the nearby trash before handing the broom back to Lou. "Sorry, again," Tink muttered, barely able to make eye contact.

Lou took the broom. "Well, I suppose no harm done," he replied, offering a small smile that put Tink at ease. Ellie walked over to the drawer and resumed sorting through the contents. All the bottles were plain and white with batch numbers written on them, along with short comments. *Batch #2 (Runny), Batch #8 (Chunky), Batch #5 (Slimy).*

Tink and Lou had begun talking about the helmet that Lou wore earlier, and how Lou believed that it might cure the hiccups. Lou explained that he often got the hiccups that would wake him up when he slept hanging upside down, so he wanted a way to fix that.

Ellie looked over at Tink and Lou discussing science and then back down at the drawer. "I don't think Lou took my sunscreen," she whispered to Jessica. "He seems to have a whole lot of his own. Do you think any of this would work for my skin type?"

Jessica shrugged. "Only one way to find out. Well, two, actually. But we won't go the 'cook you in the sun' route. Hey, Lou!"

Lou paused his conversation and turned to Jessica.

"Which one of these would work for skin type 4B?"

Lou smiled. "Any bottle will work just fine. If you can find anything after batch twelve, though, it has the best consistency."

"What do you mean, 'any bottle will work just fine?' Sunscreens don't work the same for

all vampires, you know," said Tink.

Lou gave a big smile, revealing his slightly off-white fangs. "Oh, I know," he said. "But my formula does."

Chapter Nine
A Dead End

Lou explained that he was trying to create a "one-size-fits-all" vampire sunscreen, and he had succeeded. Well, except for one minor detail.

"This stinks!" Jessica exclaimed, taking a whiff from one of the bottles in the drawer.

Lou laughed. "Yup, I've been trying for years to fix the scent, but I can't seem to change it without interfering with how it works."

Ellie's excitement faded as she took in the sour smell of the sunscreen—she finally understood why Lou always seemed to stink. It also made sense why he had been seen collecting old sunscreen bottles around town.

"Why wouldn't you just get a sunscreen shot or the special sunscreen that doesn't smell?" Ellie asked.

Lou waved his hand dismissively. "Too expensive. Why bother when I have a perfectly good sunscreen that works? The money that I save allows me to buy some science equipment every month, and I would far prefer that over smelling 'nice.' Plus, I am really close to getting the recipe to smell better." Lou pulled a piece

of paper with the sunscreen formula across the counter, and Tink readjusted his glasses as he glanced over it.

"This is genius!" Tink exclaimed.

Ellie took a whiff from batch number one and nearly fainted. "I need some fresh air," she said. Jessica was the only one listening, though, as the two boys chatted about the sunscreen formula.

Jessica and Ellie took a seat on the front step, and Ellie ran her hands over her face. "Well, that was a dead-end," she said.

"What was a dead end?" Fez asked as he walked up from the sidewalk and down the overgrown path that led to the porch. "Did you find your sunscreen?"

Ellie shook her head. "Nope. Did you drop off your dad's garlic dressing?"

Fez grinned proudly. "Sure did!" His eyes scanned the porch. "Hey, where's Tink?" Both girls silently pointed inside. Fez's eyes scanned over the old house, with its boarded windows, vines growing up the side, and a roof that looked like it might cave in at any moment.

His smile faded, and he gulped. "Tink is in there? By himself?"

"No," Jessica said matter-of-factly. Fez exhaled in relief. "He's in there with Stinky Lou--I mean, Lou."

"What!?" Fez cried.

"He's really nice," reassured Jessica. "Him and Tink seem to get along well. Turns out Lou loves science, just like Tink."

"Yup," said Ellie. "I'm sure you can go in and see Tink. It isn't so scary on the inside, well, minus the clown cat painting."

"There are cats!" Fez exclaimed, his worry instantly disappearing. He loved animals, especially cats. And dogs. And iguanas. And penguins. Okay, he loved all of them. As if on cue, the orange cat that they had seen earlier appeared in the entrance. "Oh, hi, kitty!" Fez said, perhaps a bit too loudly, as it startled the cat back inside. Seemingly fearless, Fez followed the cat. "Oh no, come back. I just want to pet you," was the last thing Ellie and Jessica heard before Fez disappeared into the house.

Jessica giggled. "He sure does like cats." But

Ellie wasn't listening. She was zoned out, staring at a big oak tree across the street. "We're going to find your sunscreen," Jessica said. She gave her friend a playful jab with her elbow. "Cheer up."

Ellie shook her head. "I think you should just ask Ava to be your partner for Jellyfish

Lake. I'm not going to be able to go." Tears welled up in Ellie's eyes.

"I don't want Ava to be my partner!" Jessica exclaimed. "You're my best friend, and I want you to come with me." A tear slipped down Ellie's cheek, and she quickly wiped it away. "I just said I would ask Ava earlier because I wanted you to find your sunscreen."

A piercing scream suddenly burst from the house.

Chapter Ten
A Piggy's Tail

Jessica and Ellie ran into the house to find everyone in the living room. They watched as two furry ears sprouted from Fez's head and a pink snout formed over his nose.

"What's happening?" said Fez, looking down at his hands turning to hooves.

Tink and Lou stood on the other side of the living room. "Don't panic," Lou commanded. He looked down at the cat brushing up against Fez. "Did you happen to pet Miss Meow Meow Face?"

Ellie couldn't help but snicker slightly. That was the best cat name she had ever heard. Fez nodded rapidly, making his pink ears flop

around. Now Tink started laughing, and Jessica too.

"Guys, this isn't funny," Fez insisted.

A small smile tugged at Lou's face as he calmly tried to explain the situation. "Miss Meow Face may have rolled around in some of my transformation powder this morning.

And while it has no effect on animals, if it was on her fur, it probably transferred to you when you pet her."

Fez scrunched his pink snout. "What did I turn into?" He looked toward the TV and caught his reflection in the darkened glass. "I'm a piglet!" he exclaimed. The whole room tried to stifle their laughter.

"Don't worry, there's an easy fix," Lou explained. "All you need to do is eat some garlic, and voila. Good as new... Unfortunately, I'm all out."

Fez's ears perked up. "I have some in my backpack!" He threw his bag on the ground and began trying to undo the zipper, but his newfound hooves made it nearly impossible.

"Here." Ellie kneeled beside Fez and helped him unzip the front compartment.

"Just grab that bottle in there and open it for me," said Fez. "It's the extra bottle of garlic dressing my dad left for me to snack on."

Ellie quickly reached in and pulled out a pair of turquoise sunglasses with bat wings on each corner.

"Hey, these are my sunglasses!" Ellie exclaimed. "Why do you have them?"

"Oh!" Fez oinked. "Someone left them at my house during the end-of-year barbecue. I meant to ask if they belonged to any of you."

Ellie tucked the glasses in her pocket and reached into the bag again. She pulled out a white bottle and popped the cap. She squeezed a bit on Fez's tongue, and they waited. After swishing the dressing in his mouth a bit, Fez swallowed, licked his lips, and let out a soft, "Mmm." He looked down at his hooves and waited for them to change—but nothing happened. "Why isn't it working?" he asked.

"Give it time," said Lou. "Even with pure garlic, it takes quite a bit for a transformation to wear off, so it will probably take a couple of hours with diluted garlic."

"Oh, okay," said Fez before letting out a small cough.

Ellie sprang to her feet and fanned Fez's garlic breath as she backed away. The white dressing bottle she held fell to the floor with a hollow plop.

Tink picked up the bottle and examined the label. "Fez, I thought you submitted your dad's entry to the contest?" He held up the bottle for everyone to see: "Fitzgerald's Garlic Dressing – Entry #21."

"I did, I mean..." Fez scrunched his face like he was trying to solve a very difficult math problem.

"If the entry bottle is here, what did you give to the judges?" Jessica asked. "The extra snack bottle?"

Ellie reached into her pocket and felt the sunglasses. She looked back at the dressing bottle, and then gasped. "Fez! I remember now! I left my sunglasses on your kitchen counter next to my sunscreen. You submitted my sunscreen to the contest!"

Fez's blue eyes began to bulge. "Oh no, the judges are going to eat your sunscreen!" He looked at the watch on his pink furry wrist. "And in only thirty minutes!"

Chapter Eleven
The Garlic Festival

The four friends ran as fast as their feet and hooves would carry them to the festival two blocks down. Since it was an outdoor event, Ellie needed something stronger than Tink's sunscreen, so she graciously accepted

when Lou offered her a bottle of the stinky formula. She smelled like a fresh fart mixed with flowers, but maybe the awful smell would mask the horrible scent of the Garlic Festival.

They waited in line to get into the gated park that was now fitted with large striped tents. Country music blared from the back speakers, and strings of colorful flags hung from all the large oak trees. Ellie turned to Fez, who was drooling over the poster for the garlic rib-eating contest. "How could you confuse

my sunscreen for dressing?" She crossed her arms over her chest.

Fez turned toward her and timidly shrugged. "It was an accident. I'm so sorry. Both bottles were on the kitchen counter, so I thought my dad made an extra bottle. I guess I got distracted by the pie they were making on the Cooking Channel... I should have been paying more attention."

Ellie sighed. "It's okay. The bottles *do* look really similar." The group went silent until they reached the front of the line. Security checked their bags and then moved their attention toward Fez the Piglet. In the rush of the situation, they had completely forgotten that it wasn't normal to walk around as a pig.

They all stood perfectly still and held their breaths as the man looked over Fez. "Turn please," requested the security guard on the left. Fez spun in a circle, which showed off the curly little tail that had sprung from the back of his pants. To their relief, both guards broke out in a smile. "That's an amazing costume!"

said the guard. He waved the group in, and everyone let out a sigh of relief.

"Well, that could have gone horribly," said Tink.

"No kidding," Jessica agreed. "I kept thinking we were about to be arrested for having a pig as a friend." Everyone but Jessica laughed. "What, Fez turned into a pig today. Anything is possible!" she argued.

The park was packed with people of all ages, many younger kids toting around balloons with pictures of garlic on them. Fez pointed over the crowd to an area near the back of the festival, where there was a large wooden stage with purple satin curtains. "That's where the competition is," he explained. "Let's go!" They all followed Fez through the thick crowd of people. Between Fez's pig features and Ellie's horrible stench, they got more than enough weird looks. Ellie nervously chewed the inside of her cheek. What if people started calling her Smelly Ellie? That would be so much worse than Scaredy Bat. Her palms began to sweat.

They hit another security checkpoint, but unfortunately this time it didn't go as well. "Excuse me," said the guard, "this is a costume-only zone." He tapped the sign that said the same thing.

"We just need to reach the food competition and we'll be out in a flash," said Ellie.

"Nope, sorry." The guard pointed to Fez. "He can come in, but you guys can't."

Jessica looked at Fez. "Go in and save the sunscreen! We'll wait here." With a quick nod, Fez agreed and ran in. The trio silently waited on a bench nearby, and Ellie nervously chewed on her fingernails. What if she couldn't go on the trip and she missed meeting Hailey Haddie? Or even worse, what if Jessica took Ava as her partner and they became best friends? A loud cheering rose from the back of the festival.

"Hey, Ellie! I thought most vampires stayed away from here. What are you guys doing at the Garlic Festival?"

Ellie looked up to a familiar, soft voice and shrieked. *Poof!*

A clown stood in front of her with messy

blue hair, a soft pink face, and overly large red lips. It turned out clowns were even creepier when they knew your name.

"Oh no. Sorry. It's just me!" The clown took off her wig to reveal her long black hair and gave her best smile. Ellie hung from a tree upside down and fluttered right side up to get a better look. Her heartbeat slowed as she recognized Ava. *Poof!*

"You almost gave me a heart attack!" Ellie exclaimed.

"Sorry..." Ava said sheepishly. "I just wanted to say hi."

"I guess this explains the creepy clown stuff in your backpack," Jessica said.

"Yeah, I decided to volunteer to get to know the town a bit better."

Honk! Honk!

The sounds of a horn blasted through the air, and Ava threw her wig back on. "That's my cue!" she explained. "See you guys later."

No sooner had Ava gone than Fez emerged from the back area with something in his hand, and Ellie's heart felt like it was thumping a million beats per minute. He ran to the group and bent over to try to catch his breath.

"Did you get it?" Tink asked.

"Where is it?" Jessica inquired.

Ellie reached down at what Fez was holding and excitedly pulled it up to get a clear view. It was... a trophy? "This isn't my sunscreen!" Ellie cried.

Chapter Twelve
We Need a Plan

F ez took a deep breath. "No, we have a problem. They are doing a blind taste test, so all the labels were peeled off the bottles, and they all look similar. There are over a hundred of them! I need help to find the sunscreen bottle."

"That still doesn't explain the trophy," said Jessica.

Fez blushed. "I may have accidentally won the best costume competition. I was the crowd favorite!"

"We need a plan," said Tink. "Well, actually we need costumes." Just then, multiple clowns emerged from a nearby tent, and a lump caught in the back of Ellie's throat. She didn't understand why clowns were a thing.

They weren't funny, just scary.

"I have an idea!" exclaimed Jessica. "Let's go." Jessica led the gang into the clown tent, which Ellie agreed to enter only after finding out it was empty. The floor was littered with clown clothes and accessories. Everything from your classic rubber chickens to rainbow-colored wigs to miles of scarves. Jessica began pulling on a costume, and Tink followed her lead. Zipping up the front of a polka-dot jumpsuit over her dress, Jessica urged Ellie to join. "Come on, you need a costume to get in."

Ellie backed as far away from the clown accessories as she could, nearly ripping the soft fabric of the tent's back wall. "There's no way I am getting near clowns or their things. You'll have to do it without me."

Jessica threw a wig on her head, her red curls still spilling out from underneath. "We can't get through that many bottles without you, Ellie. And you're most likely to recognize the sunscreen. We need you." Both Fez and Tink agreed. Jessica walked over to Ellie and put on a red nose. "See, I'm a clown now, and it's still just me. Are you really scared of your best friend?"

Ellie took a moment before answering. "I guess it's just a costume…"

"Think of Hailey Haddie," Fez added.

Ellie reluctantly agreed and pulled on a clown costume. She supposed it was just like any other Halloween costume.

"Hey, does your necklace usually glow?" Tink asked, looking over at Ellie's dragon pendant.

"Not now, Tink," said Jessica. "We have sunscreen to save!"

The three clowns and the piglet frantically ran toward the testing table, only to discover it was too late—all the bottles were empty. With the threat of heavy rain in the forecast, the festival had moved the competition up an hour.

Fez gave a sad little oink. "I thought the

competition wasn't until later," he said. "I thought we still had time...."

"Well, that's that, I guess," Ellie said with a heavy sigh. No field trip, no Hailey Haddie, no fun. This school year was turning out to be the worst.

Chapter Thirteen
Lollipop Surprise

E llie slumped down the gym wall as she watched the rest of her classmates excitedly chat about tomorrow's field trip to Jellyfish Lake—a trip that she would not be going on. She supposed being a shut-in until her new sunscreen arrived next month wasn't the worst thing in the world, though. It was far better than being called "Smelly Ellie," or whatever other nicknames her classmates would come up with. She would take Scaredy Bat over those any day.

"Ellie! Ellie!" came a small voice from the gym door. Tink, Fez, and Jessica were racing toward her.

"Oh. Hi guys," said Ellie as she tried to muster up a meek smile.

"We got you something," said Fez.

Jessica held out a purple gift bag with silver polka dots and a big pink bow.

"We think you'll like it," added Tink.

Ellie's small smile turned into a large grin as she took the bag from Jessica. She reached in and pulled out some sparkly tissue paper before finding a white-and-blue bottle. She squealed with joy. "How did you get this!? I can't believe…" Ellie trailed off as she read the label. "Fitzgerald's Garlic Dressing. Low in fat, big on taste."

"Isn't that cool!" said Fez. "My dad won the competition, all thanks to your sunscreen, and now his recipe is going to be in stores all over the country."

Ellie kept her eyes glued to the bottle, re-reading the label over and over. "That's great, Fez," she said in a monotone, almost robotic voice.

Jessica giggled. "Okay, guys, stop teasing her and give her the real gift."

Ellie looked up from the bottle for the first time. "Real gift?"

Tink unzipped his backpack and pulled out a few books, an old map, three packs of gum, and some wire. "Hold on, I know it's in here somewhere."

"Is there anything you don't have in there?" Jessica asked, placing her hands on her hips.

Ignoring the question, Tink kept digging. "Aha!" He proudly held up a simple white bottle. "*This* is your gift."

Ellie hesitantly took the bottle, her face scrunching up in confusion as she took in its plainness. Unlike the garlic dressing, this bottle didn't even have a label.

"It's Stinky Lou's sunscreen!" Fez exclaimed.

"But it doesn't smell bad anymore," added Jessica.

Ellie popped open the cap and was pleasantly surprised to be greeted with the sweet smell of lilacs. "Oh my gosh, this smells amazing! And it works?" she asked in disbelief.

"Yup!" Tink confirmed proudly. "Lou and I have been working really hard on it, and we finally figured it out. Plus, this won't just work for you; it's formulated to work for all vampires!"

Ellie's heart quickened with excitement. "Thank you so much!" She lunged toward Tink and wrapped her arms around him.

"I-I can't breathe," Tink gasped.

"Then you aren't going to like this!" Jessica jumped in to join the hug.

"Don't forget me!" said Fez, diving in too.

"Aw, look at the cute wittle group hug," taunted nearby Jack in a mocking baby voice.

They all looked around and glared at their new foe. "Jack, mind your own business," demanded Jessica.

Jack's eyes narrowed. "Make me!"

"Woah! Guys, we can all be friends." Tink reached into his backpack and started to unwrap a lollipop. Everyone looked at Tink, confused. "We can call a truce. Want to be our friend, Jack?" Jack looked down at the unwrapped blue lollipop, and the slight confusion on his face disappeared. He snatched the candy from Tink's hand and popped it in his mouth.

"Ha! Nope! I do want your candy, though. Thanks, dweeb!" And with that, Jack took off to the other side of the gym.

"Oh, I'm going to get him!" Jessica lurched forward, but Tink held her back.

"No, it's okay."

"You can't just let him steal your stuff like that, Tink!" Ellie exclaimed.

"Oh, I don't think he will be stealing anything for a while."

A loud scream sounded from the other side of the gym, and Jack emerged from a crowd of students... completely blue. Even his black curly hair was now the color of a Smurf. The

entire gym burst into laughter as Jack ran for the door.

"Oh my gosh, you turned him blue!?" Jessica exclaimed.

Tink gave a small smirk. "I told him I would when he took Fez's dressing."

As the four friends shared a laugh, Ellie couldn't believe her luck. Not only did she get to see Jack turn blue and could go on the field trip tomorrow, but she also had the best friends imaginable. Whatever mystery was in store for them next, she knew that if they worked together, nothing was unsolvable... Well, except maybe the mystery of why people liked garlic. That was something a Scaredy Bat like her would never understand.

Hi!

Did you enjoy the mystery?

I know I did!

If you want to join the team as we solve more mysteries, then leave a review!

Otherwise, we won't know if you're up for the next mystery. And when we go to solve it, you may never get to hear about it!

You can **leave a review** on Amazon, Goodreads, or wherever else you found the book.

The gang and I are excited to see you in the next mystery adventure!

Fingers crossed there's nothing scary in that one...

The mysterious adventures of Ellie Spark in

Scaredy Bat

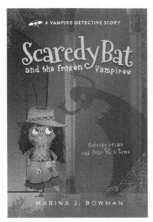

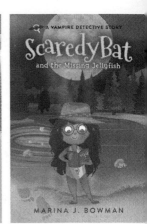

Also by Marina J. Bowman:
The Legend of Pineapple Cove

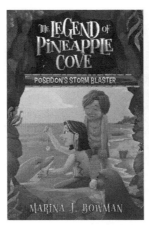

To learn more, visit marinajbowman.com

Don't miss

Book #3 in the series

Scaredy Bat and the Missing Jellyfish

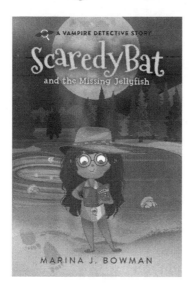

She's a smart little vampire. But she's terrified of everything. Can she summon some courage, or will her class trip be ruined?

Order Now!

scaredybat.com/book3

Are You Afraid of Clowns?

Coulrophobia [kool-ruh-foh-bee-uh] is the extreme or irrational fear of clowns. It comes from the Greek word "kolon," meaning limb or stilts, which many clowns use in circus acts, and "phobos," the Greek word for fear.

Fear Rating: Coulrophobia is one of the less common phobias in the world. People with this phobia can get panic attacks, nausea, sweat excessively, cry, or scream at the sight of clowns.

Origin: Fear of clowns likely comes from their distorted features and not knowing their true emotion or identity. Popular media has also contributed to the fear.

Fear Facts:
- The word clown comes from "klunni," the Icelandic word for clumsy person.
- Clowning is a form of entertainment in virtually every culture.
- An early form of clown was the 'fool,' which traces back to ancient Egypt.
- Fools and jesters were often the only people in court who had free speech.
- International Clown Week is celebrated each year from August 1st - 7th.
- Trained clowns must follow 8 "Clown Commandments."

Jokes: What did the egg say to the clown? You crack me up!

Fear No More! Clowns are meant to be a source of entertainment, not fear. But if you believe you suffer from coulrophobia and want help, talk to your parents or doctor about treatment options. For more fear facts, visit: scaredybat.com/book2bonus.

Suspect List

Fill in the suspects as you read, and don't worry if they're different from Ellie's suspects. When you think you've solved the mystery, fill out the "who did it" section on the next page!

Name: Write the name of your suspect

Motive: Write the reason why your suspect might have committed the crime

Access: Write the time and place you think it could have happened

How: Write the way they could have done it

Clues: Write any observations that may support the motive, access, or how

Suspect 1

Draw below

Name:	
Motive:	
Access:	
How:	
Clues:	

101

Suspect 2

Draw below

Name:
Motive:
Access:
How:
Clues:

Suspect 3

Draw below

Name:	
Motive:	
Access:	
How:	
Clues:	

Suspect 4

Draw below

Name:	
Motive:	
Access:	
How:	
Clues:	

Who Did It?

Now that you've identified all of your suspects, it's time to use deductive reasoning to figure out who actually committed the crime! Remember, the suspect must have a strong desire to commit the crime (or cause the accident) and the ability to do so.

For more detective fun, visit:
scaredybat.com/book2bonus

Name:	
Motive:	
Access:	
How:	
Clues:	

Hidden Details
Observation Sheet
-- Level One --

1. What event is advertised in the flyer that Fez was holding?
2. What unfamiliar object did Ellie find in the backpack?
3. Who did Ellie accidentally swap backpacks with?
4. What happens when vampires go out in the sun without their special sunscreen?
5. Who did Ellie see digging in the trash at her school?
6. What did Ellie find in her sister Penny's room that looked like her sunscreen?
7. What did Jack take from Fez that Ellie confused for her sunscreen?
8. What animal did Fez turn into?
9. What's the problem with Lou's sunscreen formula?
10. What did Fez submit to the Garlic Festival for the tasting competition?

Hidden Details
Observation Sheet
-- Level Two --

1. What classroom number is Ellie's homeroom?
2. What is the name of Ellie's homeroom teacher?
3. What image is on Ellie's sunscreen bottle?
4. What did Tink give Ellie to protect her from the sun to get home?
5. What did Ellie use to cover her green splotches during dinner?
6. What image was on Fez's bottle of dressing?
7. What kind of animal is featured in the paintings at Lou's house?
8. What food can help Fez turn back into a human?
9. What does Fez win a trophy for?
10. What do the kids have to dress up as to get past the second guard at the festival?

Hidden Details
Observation Sheet
-- Level Three --

1. What kind of animal is stitched onto Ava's backpack?
2. Where is the class going for their upcoming field trip?
3. How often does Ellie get a new bottle of sunscreen?
4. What image is on the purple notepad Ellie uses to take notes about suspects?
5. What is the name of the movie that Jessica's mom is acting in?
6. What is Hailey Haddie doing in the photo in Ellie's room?
7. What does Tink's homemade temporary sunscreen smell like?
8. What was Lou trying to cure with his helmet?
9. Which vampire skin type does Ellie have?
10. What does Lou's new sunscreen smell like?

For more detective fun, visit:
scaredybat.com/book2bonus

Answer Key

Level One Answers

1. The Garlic Festival
2. A clown mask
3. Ava
4. Blue spots; can drain transformation powers
5. Stinky Lou
6. Penny's sunscreen
7. Fitzgerald Garlic Dressing
8. A pig
9. It stinks
10. Ellie's sunscreen

Level Two Answers

1. 302
2. Mr Bramble
3. Sun with a straw hat and red sunglasses
4. Tinfoil
5. A purple scarf
6. A yellow garlic head wearing red sunglasses
7. A cat
8. Garlic
9. Costume contest
10. Clowns

Level Three Answers

1. Lion
2. Jellyfish Lake
3. Once a month
4. Silver skeleton key
5. Vampires in Paradise
6. Chewing a pen cap as she made a list of suspects
7. Black licorice
8. Hiccups
9. Skin type 4B
10. Lilacs

Questions for Discussion

1. What did you enjoy about this book?
2. What are some of the major themes of this story?
3. Who was your favorite character? What did you like about him/her?
4. How did the characters use their strengths to solve the mystery together?
5. Have you ever experienced bullying? What happened?
6. What fears did the characters express in the book? When have you been afraid? How have you dealt with your fears?
7. What is your favorite red colored food?
8. What other books, shows, or movies does this story remind you of?
9. What do you think will happen in the next book in the series?
10. If you could talk to the author, what is one question you would ask her?

For more discussion questions, visit:
scaredybat.com/book2bonus

About the Author

Marina J. Bowman is a writer and explorer who travels the world searching for wildly fantastical stories to share with her readers. Ever since she was a child, she has been fascinated with uncovering long lost secrets and chasing the mythical, magical, and supernatural. For her current story, Marina is investigating a charming town in the northern US, where vampires and humans live in harmony.

Marina enjoys sailing, flying, and nearly all other forms of transportation. She never strays far from the ocean for long, as it brings her both inspiration and peace. She stays away from the spotlight to maintain privacy and ensure the more unpleasant secrets she uncovers don't catch up with her.

As a matter of survival, Marina nearly always communicates with the public through her representative, Devin Cowick. Ms. Cowick is an entrepreneur who shares Marina's passion for travel and creative storytelling and is the co-founder of Code Pineapple.

Marina's last name is pronounced baʊmən, and rhymes with "now then."

Made in the USA
Coppell, TX
12 November 2021

65649758R00076